Political Leaders

BLACK HISTORY MAKERS

Adam Sutherland

PowerKiDS press
New York

Published in 2012 by The Rosen Publishing Group, Inc.
29 East 21st Street, New York, NY 10010

Copyright © 2012 Wayland/The Rosen Publishing Group, Inc.

All rights reserved. No part of this book may be reproduced in any form without permission in writing from the publisher, except by a reviewer.

Editor: Katie Woolley, Jennifer Way
Designer: Tim Mayer, MayerMedia
Consultant: Mia Morris, Black History Month Web Site

Picture Acknowledgments: Cover, title page, pp. 7, 16, 20, 21, 23 (bottom center), 23 (top left) Shutterstock; pp. 3, 11 Alexander Joe/AFP/Getty Images; p. 5 Bettmann/Corbis; p. 6 Mary Evans Picture Libraryl p. 8 Hulton Archive/Getty Images; p. 9 W. Robert Moore/National Geographic Society/Corbis; p. 10 Siphiwe Sibeko/Reuters/Corbis; p. 12 William Campbell/Sygma/Corbis; p. 13 Photoshot; p. 14 Leif Skoogfors/Corbis; p. 15 Don Hogan Charles/New York Times Co./Getty Images; p. 17 Orlando Barria/EFE/Corbis; p. 18 Jason Reed/Reuters/Corbis; p. 19 Bru Garcia/AFP/Getty Images; p. 23 (top center) Back Page Images/Rex Features; p. 23 (top right) Neilson Barnard/Getty Images; p. 23 (bottom right) Alisdair MacDonald/Rex Features; p. 23 (bottom left) © 2004 TopFoto/UPP/TopFoto.co.uk.

Library of Congress Cataloging-in-Publication Data

Sutherland, Adam.
  Political leaders / by Adam Sutherland. — 1st ed.
    p. cm. — (Black history makers)
  Includes index.
  ISBN 978-1-4488-6639-7 (lib. bdg.) — ISBN 978-1-4488-7056-1 (pbk.) — ISBN 978-1-4488-7057-8 (6-pack)
  1. Politicians—Africa—Biography—Juvenile literature. 2. Politicians—Africa—History—Juvenile literature. 3. Political leadership—Africa—History—Juvenile literature. 4. African American politicians—Biography—Juvenile literature. 5. African American politicians—History—Juvenile literature. 6. Blacks—Political activity—History—Juvenile literature. I. Title.
  DT18.S87 2012
  324.2092'396—dc23
                              2011029819

Manufactured in Malaysia

WEB SITES:

Due to the changing nature of Internet links, PowerKids Press has developed an online list of Web sites related to the subject of this book. This site is updated regularly. Please use this link to access the list:
powerkidslinks.com/blackhist/political/

CPSIA Compliance Information: Batch #WW2102PK: For Further Information contact Rosen Publishing, New York, New York at 1-800-237-9932

CONTENTS

Making History — 4

Queen Nzinga
Freedom Fighter — 6

Toussaint Louverture
Revolutionary Leader — 7

Haile Selassie
The African Modernizer — 8

Nelson Mandela
The Symbol of Hope — 10

Kenneth Kaunda
Fighter for African Independence — 12

Shirley Chisholm
The Educator — 14

Kofi Annan
The World's Peacemaker — 16

Ellen Johnson Sirleaf
Liberia's First Woman President — 18

Condoleezza Rice
The Special Advisor — 19

Barack Obama
The United States' First Black President — 20

Other Rulers and Leaders — 22

Timeline — 23

Legacy — 23

Glossary — 24

Index — 24

J
324.20
SUT

Making History

From the sixteenth to the nineteenth centuries, millions of Africans were transported from west and central Africa to work as slaves all over the world. Many were sent to **plantations** in the southern United States and on the islands of the Caribbean.

Many people opposed slavery and it was fought around the globe. Leaders like Queen Nzinga in Angola (page 6) and Toussaint Louverture in Haiti (page 7) fought not only to end slavery but also to try to earn their countries' freedom.

African Independence

Between the 1880s and the start of World War I in 1914, much of Africa was ruled by European countries. Up until the 1950s and 1960s, white **minorities** controlled African governments. These European **colonizers** would sell a country's natural resources such as copper, cotton, rubber, and cocoa and keep the profit for themselves.

Kenneth Kaunda (page 12) helped Zambia escape this colonial rule and established a well-governed country with an outstanding education system. When Kaunda came to power in 1964 there were 100 university graduates in Zambia. By the time he retired in 1991 there were 12,000!

Fighting Apartheid

In 1948, the National Party was elected in South Africa, bringing with it their policy of **apartheid**, a system of legalized **racial discrimination**. The black **majority** in the country were forced to live in certain areas, work in certain jobs, study at certain schools, and even eat in certain restaurants that the government decided were suitable.

In a protest against apartheid in South Africa, these South African people have taken over a train compartment marked "Europeans Only."

Nelson Mandela (page 10) battled the white apartheid government, spending 27 years in prison for fighting this unfair system. As a free man, he helped to end apartheid and became South Africa's first **democratically elected** President.

While these rulers and leaders have lived and ruled across the world, they have all worked for freedom, independence, and the well-being of their fellow men and women.

Queen Nzinga
Freedom Fighter

In the sixteenth century, Portuguese slave traders set up camp in the Congo region in southwestern Africa. They stole land from the locals to build their bases, and captured men, women, and children to work and sell as slaves. They used mercenaries, or professional soliders, from the Imbangala tribe to stop resistance from local forces. The person who led the fiercest opposition to the Portuguese and their mercenaries was Queen Nzinga.

Name: Nzinga Mbande

Born: circa 1583, Kingdom of Ndongo (today's Angola)

Died: December 17, 1663

Position: Queen of the Ndongo and Matamba Kingdoms of the Mbundu tribes in southwestern Africa

Awards and achievements: Brought peace to Angola, resettled former slaves and united her country.

Interesting fact: When she first met the Portuguese governor, Nzinga used one of her handmaidens as her seat rather than take an inferior, standing position.

Queen Nzinga is still remembered in Angola for her intelligence, political skills, and brilliant military tactics.

Going into Battle

In 1622, Nzinga's brother Ngola Mbandi tried to get these slave traders to stop fighting against local forces and to release many of the slaves they held. The Portuguese agreed but soon broke their promises. When Ngola committed suicide in despair, Nzinga took his place as ruler of the Mbundu people and took the title of Queen of Andongo.

Nzinga's Legacy

Nzinga declared war against the Portuguese in 1624, eventually forcing Portugal to sign a **peace treaty** in 1657. This allowed Nzinga to focus on rebuilding her war-damaged country and resettling former slaves. She died peacefully in 1663 at the age of 80.

Toussaint Louverture
Revolutionary Leader

Toussaint Louverture was a former slave who worked on one of Haiti's plantations before being freed at the age of 33. He was determined to end slavery in Haiti and led **guerrilla troops** into battle against British, Spanish, and French forces many times. He helped bring about the **abolition** of slavery, and became Haiti's leader in 1801.

Imprisonment

The French President Napoleon Bonaparte sent troops to regain control of Haiti in 1802. Louverture signed a peace treaty with France but the French falsely accused him of plotting against Napoleon.

Name: Francois-Dominique Toussaint Louverture

Born: May 20, 1743, Saint-Domingue, Haiti

Died: April 7, 1803

Position: Leader of the Haitian Revolution, 1791–1804

Awards and achievements: Abolished slavery and secured Haitian control of the colony.

Interesting fact: English poet William Wordsworth wrote a poem about Louverture in 1803 called "To Toussaint L'Ouverture."

Louverture was arrested and taken to France where he died in prison in 1803. Haitians continued to resist French rule, and by 1804, French troops withdrew from Haiti. Haiti was now and independent country, and Louverture was a national hero.

Toussaint Louverture was a slave who worked as a driver and horse trainer before being freed.

MAKING HISTORY

Toussaint Louverture was the leader of the first ever successful slave **revolution**. Through his efforts, Haiti became the first free black **republic** in the world when it declared independence on January 1, 1804.

Haile Selassie
The African Modernizer

Name: Tafari Makonnen

Born: July 23, 1892, Ejersa Goro, Ethiopia

Died: August 27, 1975

Position: Emperor of Ethiopia 1930–1974

Awards and achievements: Introduced his country's first written **constitution** and fought for a fairer division of wealth.

Interesting fact: Brought electricity to Ethiopia, first in the palace and then into other buildings.

A portrait of the emperor taken in the 1950s. Selassie celebrated 25 years in power in 1955.

A Royal Heir

Haile Selassie was born Tafari Makonnen. The heir to an Ethiopian royal family, his mother was daughter of the ruler of the Wollo province and his father the governor of Harar. His father died in 1906 when Selassie was 14 years of age and the young man immediately became governor of Selale and Sidamo provinces. Over the next few years Selassie's experience and influence grew and when Empress Zewditu died in 1930, he was crowned Emperor of Ethiopia.

In Power

As soon as he became emperor, Selassie set out to make his country a better governed and fairer country than it had been in the past. He introduced the first written constitution in 1931, which saw **democratic** rule in the country for the first time. Unfortunately, his efforts were put on hold when Italy invaded Ethiopia and, in May 1936, Selassie and his family were forced into **exile**. He returned home when his country was liberated in 1941.

8

> *Until the color of a man's skin is of no more significance than the color of his eyes... there [will be] wars.*
>
> Haile Selassie

Haile Selassie and Queen Menen pose in their robes in 1931, not long after he was crowned emperor in November 1930.

Lasting Legacy

After the World War II (1939–1945), Ethiopia became a **founding member** of the United Nations. Selassie fought for a fairer division of land and wealth in his country. His planned **economic reforms** were often met with strong opposition from the country's landowners.

The End of His Reign

During celebrations for his 25 years in power in 1955, he unveiled a revised, more democratic constitution. Selassie was forced from power in a military uprising led by a group called the Derg in September 1974. He was imprisoned by the Derg and died in August 1975.

Nelson Mandela
The Symbol of Hope

Nelson Mandela's great-grandfather was king of the Thembu people and his father was chief of the town of Mvezo. The young Mandela was the first in his family to receive an education and he started a degree at Fort Hare University. However, Nelson was asked to leave after one year because he was involved in a student protest against racist university selection policies. He started work at a Johannesburg law firm.

Name: Nelson Rolihlahla Mandela

Born: July 18, 1918, Mvezo, South Africa

Position: President of South Africa 1994–1999

Awards and achievements: The first democratically elected South African President.

Interesting fact: While Mandela was in prison he was offered freedom if he would say he rejected the use of violence to oppose aparthied. He refused this offer.

Former South African President Mandela attends an African National Congress (ANC) election rally in Johannesburg before the 2009 elections.

Life in Politics

After the 1948 election victory by the National Party, who supported apartheid, Mandela became actively involved in politics and the rights of black people in South Africa. Apartheid is an African word meaning "separation" or "apartness." It is the name that South Africa's white government from 1948–1990 used to describe its discrimination against the country's non-white majority. Black people were denied a proper education, forced to live in specific areas away from white people, and only allowed to do certain jobs.

> "I detest racialism... whether it comes from a black man or a white man."
> Nelson Mandela

Nelson Mandela and his then-wife Winnie salute the cheering crowds following his release from Victor Verster prison in February 1990.

In Prison

In 1961, Mandela became leader of Umkhonto we Sizwe (meaning "Spear of the Nation"), the armed wing of the African National Congress (ANC). He coordinated sabotage campaigns against military and government targets. In 1962, he was arrested and sentenced to life in prison. Mandela served most of his sentence on Robben Island. Prisoners were separated by color, with black prisoners receiving the fewest rations. While he was in prison, Mandela earned a law degree through a **correspondence course**.

Walk to Freedom

South African President F.W. de Klerk released Mandela from prison in 1990. Mandela was immediately elected president of the ANC. He and de Klerk worked together to bring apartheid to a peaceful end and to organize the country's first multiracial elections. The ANC won and Mandela became the country's president. He retired from politics in 1999, but still works tirelessly for several human rights organizations.

MAKING HISTORY

For his commitment to bringing apartheid to an end and for his leadership of the ANC after his release from prison, Nelson Mandela was jointly awarded the Nobel Peace Prize in 1993 together with President F.W. de Klerk.

Kenneth Kaunda
Fighter for African Independence

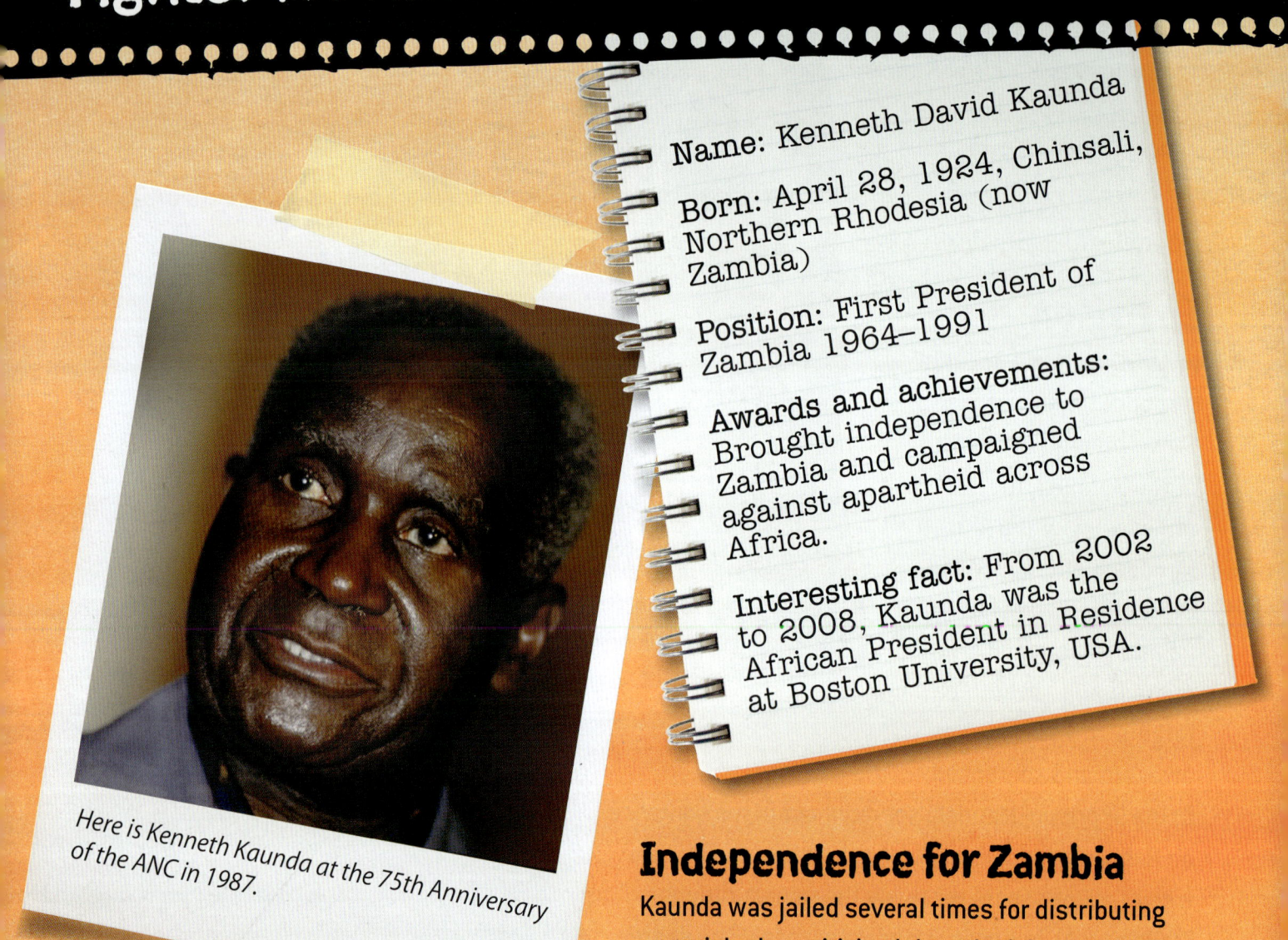

Name: Kenneth David Kaunda

Born: April 28, 1924, Chinsali, Northern Rhodesia (now Zambia)

Position: First President of Zambia 1964–1991

Awards and achievements: Brought independence to Zambia and campaigned against apartheid across Africa.

Interesting fact: From 2002 to 2008, Kaunda was the African President in Residence at Boston University, USA.

Here is Kenneth Kaunda at the 75th Anniversary of the ANC in 1987.

Early Life

Kenneth Kaunda was the youngest of eight children and grew up in Northern Rhodesia, a British colony that was ruled by a minority white government. As a young man, Kaunda worked as a teacher, a soldier, and a miner. In 1951, Kanuda decided to make his life's work aiding the struggle for African independence.

Independence for Zambia

Kaunda was jailed several times for distributing materials that criticized the colonial government and for being leader of the banned Zambian African National Congress (ZANC). This only encouraged Kanuda to work harder to reach his goal of independence for all African countries.

While Kaunda was in prison, fellow ZANC members formed the United National Independence Party (UNIP). When Kaunda was released in 1960 he was elected president of UNIP. In January 1964, when UNIP won the country's pre-independence election, Kaunda became prime minister.

Kenneth Kaunda was a strong and fearless leader who led his country to independence.

Zambia's Leader

In October 1964, the country gained independence and took the name Zambia, from the Zambezi river, which runs through the country. Kaunda became the first president of Zambia and began the task of building a new country, investing in primary education and fighting to take back control of the country's important mineral rights, especially copper, from foreign companies like the British South Africa Company (BSAC).

African Legacy

President Kaunda's opposition to white governments in Southern Rhodesia (now Zimbabwe), South Africa, and South-West Africa (now Namibia) meant that Zambia was often attacked by foreign rebel forces. The economy also suffered from falling world copper prices and is still one of the poorest countries in the world today. Kaunda's lasting legacy was in bringing independence to Zambia. Since retiring from office in 1991 he has devoted his life to fighting HIV and AIDS in Africa.

MAKING HISTORY

Kenneth Kaunda was an early fighter for African democracy. Nelson Mandela believes that Kaunda and Zambia were very important role models when he became president of South Africa. Mandela was able to learn from Zambia's developing democracy, both from what they did right and what they did wrong, to help South Africa emerge from its own white minority rule.

Shirley Chisholm
The Educator

Name: Shirley Anita St. Hill Chisholm

Born: November 30, 1924, Brooklyn, New York

Died: January 1, 2005

Position: U.S. congresswoman 1969–1983

Awards and achievements: The first African American woman elected to Congress.

Interesting fact: Chisholm has had songs written about her by rappers Outkast and Method Man.

Shirley Chisholm addressed a crowd on the subject of racism in the Armed Forces in 1971.

Getting an Education

Shirley Chisholm was born in New York City to West Indian parents. She was sent to live with her grandmother in Barbados from the ages of 3 to 10, because her parents believed that the American education system was inadequate and they wanted their daughter to benefit from a traditional, British-style education. Chisholm returned to New York in 1934 and often credited those years in Barbados as the foundation of her success.

Working Life

In 1946, Chisholm took a degree at Brooklyn College and then earned an MA in elementary education at Columbia University in 1952. From 1953 to 1959 Chisholm worked as director of Hamilton-Madison Child Care Center. From 1959 to 1964, she was a consultant for local government.

> "I've always met more discrimination being a woman than being black."
> — Shirley Chisholm

In Office

New York City in the 1950s and 1960s struggled to provide access to good education and services for its poorest residents. Having worked in education and child care for 14 years, Chisholm wanted to address these problems and this led her to run for a seat in the U.S. Congress. In 1968, she was elected to represent New York's 12th Congressional District. She supported employment and education programs and the expansion of day care so that parents could afford to return to work.

Running for President

In 1972, Chisholm became the first woman to run for the Democratic Party's presidential nomination as well as the first African American candidate of a major party to run for president. She campaigned in 12 states and received 152 first-ballot votes but failed to beat fellow candidate George McGovern. Nevertheless, she was a ground-breaking politician whose influence can still be felt today.

MAKING HISTORY

Shirley Chisholm fought for freedom and equality in education and in the workplace. During her time in office, every colleague she hired for her congressional team was a woman and half of them were African Americans.

Here is Shirley Chisholm in 1972 announcing her intention to run for the Democratic Party's presidential nomination.

Kofi Annan
The World's Peacemaker

An Inspiring Past

Annan's father was a nobleman of the Fante tribe in Ghana and his uncle and both of his grandfathers were tribal chiefs. The young Annan was sent to a Methodist boarding school from 1954 to 1957. He said it was there that he was taught "that suffering anywhere concerns people everywhere."

Names: Kofi Atta Annan

Born: April 8, 1938, Kumasi, Gold Coast (now Ghana)

Position: Secretary-General of the United Nations 1997–2006

Awards and achievements: Joint winner of 2001 Nobel Peace Prize.

Interesting fact: In Ghana, children are named after the day of the week on which they are born. Kofi means "Friday."

Education

In 1958, Kofi Annan began a degree in economics in Ghana. In 1961, he received a scholarship from the Ford Foundation that allowed him to complete his studies in the United States. Annan received a graduate degree in International Relations in Geneva, Switzerland, in 1962.

Kofi Annan has spent his life campaigning for peace throughout the world.

> "We may have different religions, different languages, different colored skin, but we all belong to one human race."
>
> *Kofi Annan*

UN Career

Between 1987 and 1996, Annan worked for the United Nations (UN) as Assistant Secretary-General in three different areas. One of his biggest regrets from these years was not being able to stop the Rwandan genocide in 1994, in which members of the majority Hutu tribe turned on the minority ruling Tutsi tribe, killing an estimated 800,000 people over the course of 100 days. He swore that in the future he would do everything in his power to persuade the world to act more quickly to prevent the loss of innocent lives.

MAKING HISTORY

When the United Nations was formed in 1945, the position of Secretary-General was described by President Franklin Delano Roosevelt as a "world moderator," or someone who would speak out and play an important role in keeping world peace. As the UN grew to today's 192 member countries, the Secretary-General's role now includes a large number of global issues. Kofi Annan was influential in raising the profile of the job in the eyes of the world. He persuaded member countries that they had a responsibility to the world as a whole and not just to their own nations.

Position of Power

As Secretary-General, Annan was persuasive and compassionate. He saw his responsibility as acting as the world's conscience. He used UN troops to try and stop fighting everywhere from Kosovo to Darfur. He raised funds and awareness to reduce the spread of AIDS, combat diabetes, and promote women's rights.

Kofi Annan was decorated with the Dominican Republic's Order of Duarte, Sanchez, and Mella, shown here, in 2006. It is the country's highest honor.

Ellen Johnson Sirleaf
Liberia's First Woman President

A Good Beginning

Ellen Johnson Sirleaf's parents were both from prominent Liberian families, and they pushed their daughter to develop an international outlook. She studied economics at the college of West Africa from 1948 to 1955. She then traveled to the United States in 1961 to continue her studies, eventually earning a degree in economics at the University of Colorado. She followed that with two years at Harvard University, where she earned an MA in economics and public policy in 1971.

Name: Ellen Johnson Sirleaf

Born: October 29, 1938, Monrovia, Liberia

Position: President of Liberia 2006–present

Awards and achievements: First elected female leader in Africa. Joint recipient of 2011 Nobel Peace Prize.

Interesting fact: Sirleaf's story was told in the 2008 documentary entitled *Pray the Devil Back to Hell*.

Sirleaf returned to Liberia to work as Assistant Minister of Finance from 1972 to 1973, and then as Minister of Finance from 1979 to 1980. In 1980, the government was overthrown by military leaders and the president and several cabinet members were killed. Sirleaf escaped to Kenya and then to the United States.

Becoming President

The military coup led to two civil wars that devastated Liberia's economy and killed thousands of people. When a peace treaty was signed in 2003 between the government and rebel groups, Sirleaf returned to Liberia and won the presidential election in 2005. In 2011, Sirleaf was a joint recipient of the Nobel Peace Prize for her work to promote women's rights.

As president, Sirleaf is working to improve social conditions and has made elementary education free and compulsory for all children.

Condoleezza Rice
The Special Advisor

A Concert Dream
Condoleezza Rice was born into a family where education, music, and the arts were extremely important. Her father was a minister and her mother taught music and public speaking. Rice started learning French, music, and ballet at three years old. At 15, she began taking lessons to be a concert pianist but during college decided to focus on her education.

Studies
Rice finished her degree in political science at 19. As soon she completed her Ph.D in 1981, she was hired by Stanford University as a Professor of Political Science. She was a specialist on the Soviet Union and one of her lectures in 1985 caught the attention of U.S. National Security Advisor Brent Scowcroft.

Moving into Politics
When George H.W. Bush became president in 1989, Scowcroft brought Rice to the White House to help develop U.S. government policy toward the Soviet Union. She returned to Stanford to teach in 1991, but maintained her political connections, taking a one-year leave of absence to help with George W. Bush's 2000 presidential campaign. During George W. Bush's two terms, Rice first serverd as National Security Advisor and then as Secretary of State. In 2009, she returned to Stanford University to continue her career as a professor.

Name: Condoleezza Rice

Born: November 14, 1954, Birmingham, Alabama

Position: U.S. National Security Advisor 2001–2005, U.S. Secretary of State 2005–2009

Awards and achievements: First African American woman U.S. Secretary of State.

Interesting fact: Her name comes from the Italian musical expression con dolcezza meaning "with sweetness."

After working for the United States' government, Condoleezza Rice is again working at Stanford University as a political science professor.

Barack Obama
The United States' First Black President

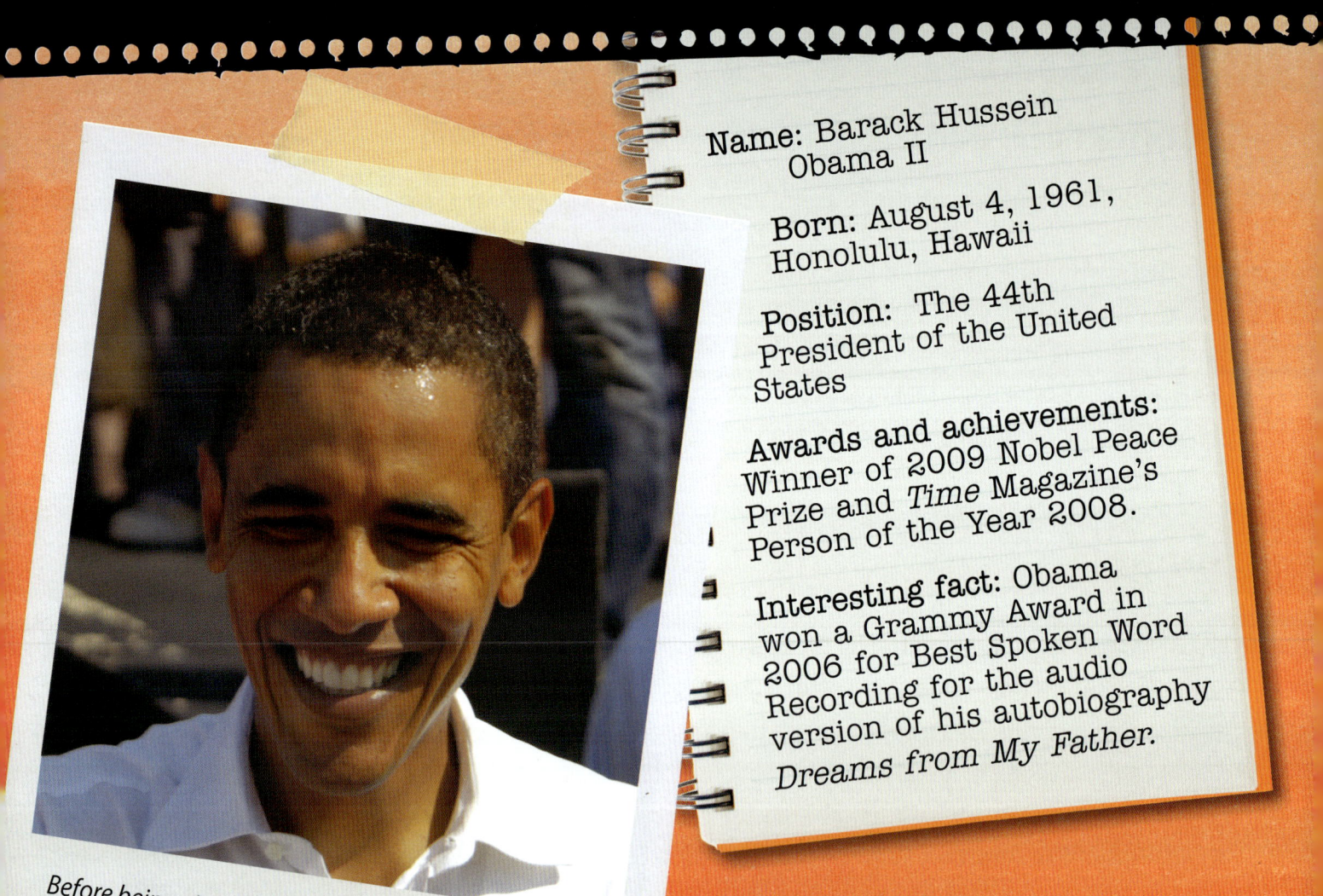

Name: Barack Hussein Obama II

Born: August 4, 1961, Honolulu, Hawaii

Position: The 44th President of the United States

Awards and achievements: Winner of 2009 Nobel Peace Prize and *Time* Magazine's Person of the Year 2008.

Interesting fact: Obama won a Grammy Award in 2006 for Best Spoken Word Recording for the audio version of his autobiography *Dreams from My Father*.

Before being elected to the Senate, Barack Obama taught constitutional law at the University of Chicago Law School from 1992 to 2004.

> " There is not a black America and a white America... there's the United States of America. "
>
> Barack Obama

The Early Years

Barack Obama was born in Hawaii to a white American mother and a black Kenyan father. His parents divorced in 1964, when Obama Senior left Hawaii to study at Harvard University. His mother remarried to Indonesian student Lolo Soetoro and the family moved to Jakarta, Indonesia. Obama lived there from 1967 to 1971, before returning to live with his maternal grandparents in Hawaii to attend the fifth through twelfth grade.

As the first black president of the publication, Obama started to gain national media attention. He was offered a publishing contract to write a book on race relations that became his best-selling autobiography *Dreams from My Father*, published in 1995.

Becoming President

Obama's personal beliefs have always included helping people exercise their ridghts, such as the right to vote, the right to housing, the right to earn a living, and the right to healthcare. These commitments have been constant through the time he was elected to the Illinois Senate in 1996, to the United States Senate in 2004 and most of all when he was elected president in 2008.

President Obama's abilities as an inspirational public speaker helped win his election campaign.

Studying Hard

Obama was always ambitious and hard-working. He won a place at the prestigious Columbia University to study political science and, after graduating in 1983, worked in community housing projects in Chicago, before attending Harvard Law School. At Harvard, he was elected president of the *Harvard Law Review*, a long-standing and well-respected journal that was published by Harvard Law School's best students.

MAKING HISTORY

As president, Barack Obama has passed a number of important and historic laws. To combat global recession, he passed The American Recovery and Reinvestment Act (2009), pumping $787 billion into the United States economy. Perhaps most important though, is the Affordable Health Care for America Act (2009), which will for the first time give 36 million Americans the right to free and subsidized health care.

Other Rulers and Leaders

Kwame Nkrumah (1909–1972)

Kwame was the leader of Ghana and the Gold Coast from 1952 to 1966. He campaigned against British colonial rule in his country and spent time in prison for his actions. His Convention People's Party (CPP) won the country's first free election, making Nkrumah president. He modernized Ghana, helping it to become one of the wealthiest countries in Africa.

Julius Kambarage Nyerere (1922–1999)

He became Tanganyika's first prime minister in 1961 and president a year later when the country became a republic. Nyerere was instrumental in the birth of Tanzania, when the islands of Zanzibar united with mainland Tanganyika in 1964.

Colin Powell (1937–)

Powell was the first African American Secretary of State (2001–2005). Born in New York City to Jamaican immigrant parents, Powell was a professional soldier for 35 years. He was the Secretary of State in George W. Bush's administration and remains active in public and political life.

Jacob Zuma (1942–)

Zuma became the President of South Africa in 2009. He joined the ANC at 17 and was arrested in 1963 for conspiring to overthrow the apartheid government. Zuma spent ten years in prison, then lived in exile in Mozambique, and returnined to South Africa in 1990. Zuma became president of the ANC in 2007 before becoming South Africa's president two years later.

Baroness Valerie Amos (1954–)

Amos was leader of the United Kingdom's House of Lords from 2003 to 2007. Born in Guyana and educated in England, Valerie became Chief Executive of the Equal Opportunities Commission in 1989, advising the South African government on human rights and employment law. As leader of the House of Lords, she often spoke out about international development and foreign affairs.

Dr. Susan Elizabeth Rice (1964–)

Born in Washington, D.C., Rice became the United States Ambassador to the United Nations in 2009. She won scholarships to Stanford University, then Oxford University in England, where she studied history and international relations. Rice became Assistant Secretary of State for African Affairs in 1997 and worked to help Africa compete in the global economy. A foreign policy advisor to Barack Obama during his election campaign, Rice is the first black woman United States representative to the United Nations.

Timeline

1624 Nzinga becomes Queen of Andongo

1776 Toussaint Louverture freed from slavery

1930 Haile Selassie crowned Emperor of Ethiopia

1957 Kwame Nkrumah becomes prime minister of Ghana

1964 Kenneth Kaunda becomes president of independent Zambia

1964 Julius Nyerere becomes first president of Tanzania

1968 Shirley Chisholm becomes the first black woman elected to United States Congress

1994 Nelson Mandela becomes South Africa's first black president

2000 Condoleezza Rice named United States National Security Advisor

2001 Kofi Annan and the United Nations receive the Nobel Peace Prize

2001 Colin Powell becomes the first African American United States Secretary of State

2003 Valerie Amos becomes leader of the House of Lords

2005 Ellen Johnson Sirleaf becomes Liberia's first female president

2008 Barack Obama is elected president of the United States

2009 Jacob Zuma becomes president of South Africa

2009 Susan Rice becomes United States Ambassador to the United Nations

2011 Ellen Johnson Sirleaf receives the Nobel Peace Prize.

Legacy

The legacies of the rulers and leaders in this book live on, not only in their achievements but also through the work of their families and followers:

The Nelson Mandela Foundation
www.nelsonmandela.org/index.php
Mandela established the Foundation after he retired as president of South Africa. The Foundation focuses on spreading peace and unity.

The Global Fund
www.theglobalfund.org
Kofi Annan founded this charity to fight AIDS, tuberculosis (TB) and malaria. It is the world's largest funder of programs to combat TB and malaria, and provides 20 percent of world funding to combat AIDS.

The Kenneth Kaunda Children of Africa Foundation
http://www.facebook.com/group.php?gid=87179224121
Set up to fight the AIDS epidemic in Africa and to help the children orphaned by the disease.

Glossary

abolition (a-buh-LIH-shun) To have ended or done away with.

apartheid (uh-PAR-tyd) The South African National Party's official government policy of racial separation, or 'segregation', from 1948–1990.

colonizer (KAH-luh-nyz-ur) A person who settles in a country a long way from their own homeland, but maintains ties with it.

constitution (kon-stih-TOO-shun) The rules or principles on which a country is governed or ruled.

correspondence course (kor-ih-SPON-dens KORS) A method of studying by post. Teachers send out work assignments and students send back their essays for marking.

democratic (deh-muh-KRA-tik) For the benefit of everyone.

democratically elected (deh-muh-KRA-tik-lee ee-LEK-tid) A government or leader who is chosen to lead a country or group based on a system of voting that allows everyone a vote.

economic reform (eh-kuh-NAH-mik rih-FORM) Improvements or changes to the economy of a country, for example how the wealth is divided between rich and poor.

exile (EG-zyl) A prolonged, usually enforced, absence from one's home or country.

founding member (FOWND-ing MEM-bur) One of the first or original members who helps to set up or establish an organization.

guerrilla troops (guh-RIL-uh TROOPS) A part-time, politically motivated armed force that fights against stronger regular forces.

majority (muh-JOR-ih-tee) A group that is different racially or politically, for example, from a smaller group of which it is a part.

minority (my-NOR-ih-tee) A group that is different racially or politically, for example, from a larger group of which it is a part.

peace treaty (PEES TREE-tee) An agreement to end a war or conflict.

plantation (plan-TAY-shun) A large farm or estate where crops such as rubber or sugar cane are grown.

racial discrimination (RAY-shul dis-krih-muh-NAY-shun) The unfair treatment of a person or racial group based on prejudice.

republic (rih-PUH-blik) A form of government in which the people or their elected representatives hold power.

revolution (reh-vuh-LOO-shun) The overthrow of a government or political system by the people.

Index

A
Africa 4, 12, 18, 22
African National Congress (ANC) 10, 11, 22
Amos, Valerie Ann 22
Angola 6
Annan, Kofi 16–17
apartheid 5, 10, 11, 12, 22

B
Barbados 14
Bonaparte, Napoleon 7

C
Chisholm, Shirley 14–15
Convention People's Party 22

D
De Klerk, F.W. 11
Democratic Party 15

E
Ethopia 8

F
France 7

G
Ghana 16, 22
Grammy Award 20

H
Haiti 5
Hawaii 20

I
Italy 8

K
Kaunda, Kenneth 5, 12–13

L
Liberia 18
Louverture, Toussaint 4, 7

M
Mandela, Nelson 5, 10–11, 13

N
National Party 5
Nkrumah, Kwame 22
Nobel Peace Prize 11, 16, 20
Nyerere, Julius 22
Nzinga, Queen 4, 6

O
Obama, Barack 20–21

P
plantation 4, 7
Powell, Colin 22

R
Robben Island 11
Rice, Condoleezza 19
Rice, Dr. Susan Elizabeth 22

S
Selassie, Haile 8–9
Sirleaf Johnson, Ellen 18
slave 4, 6, 7
slave revolution 7
slave trader 6
South Africa 5, 10, 13, 22

U
United Kingdom (UK) 22
United National Independence Party 12
United Nations (UN) 9, 17, 22
United States 4, 14, 18, 19, 20, 21, 22

Z
Zambezi river 13
Zambia 12, 13
Zambian African National Congress (ZANC) 12
Zuma, Jacob 22

24